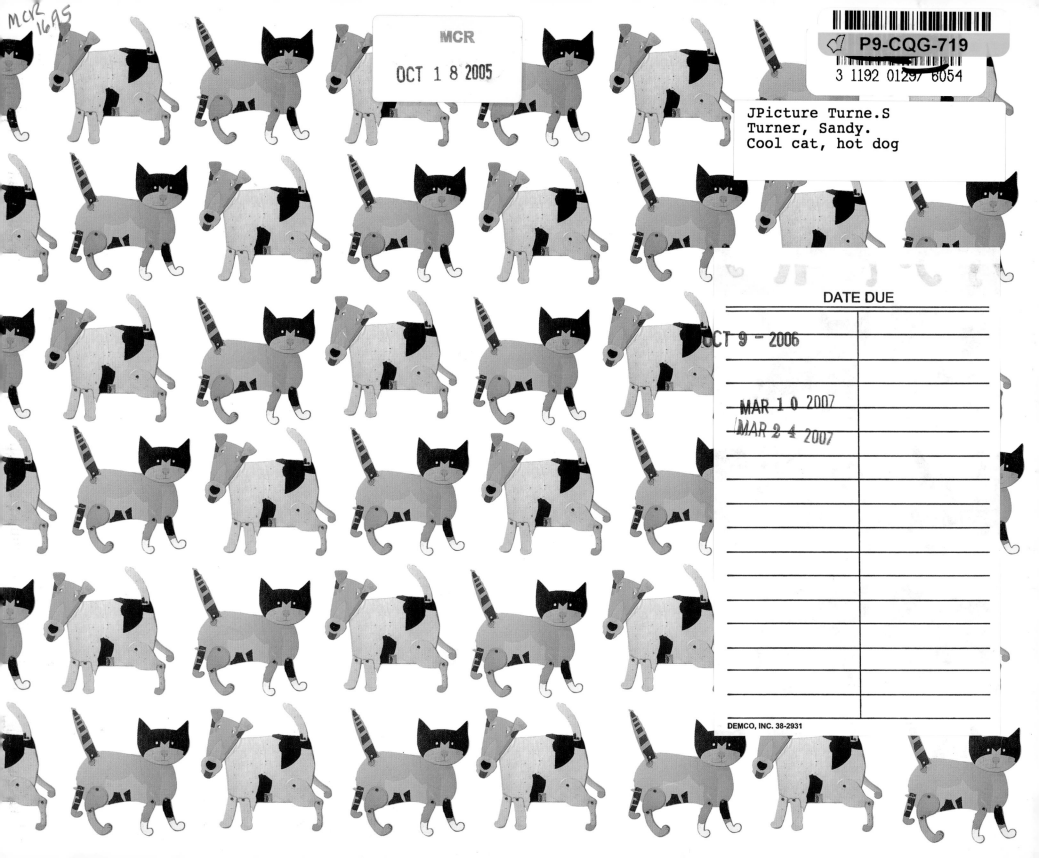

THE DO NOT
COPY - CAT
SCRAP - BOOK

BeWARE of THE
D   O   G

Dedication:

My tale is longer, Caitlyn Dlouhy

Atheneum Books for Young Readers ● An imprint of Simon & Schuster Children's Publishing Division ● 1230 Avenue of the Americas ● New York, New York 10020 ● Copyright © 2005 by Sandy Turner ● All rights reserved, including the right of reproduction in whole or in part in any form. ● Book design by Daniel Roode ● The text for this book is set in Harting. ● The illustrations for this book are rendered in cut paper, pencil, and collage. ● Manufactured in China ● First Edition ● 10 9 8 7 6 5 4 3 2 1 ● Library of Congress Cataloging-in-Publication Data ● Turner, Sandy. ● Cool cat, hot dog / Sandy Turner — 1st ed. ● p. cm. ● Summary: A cat and a dog have a good-natured argument about their differences. ● ISBN 0-689-84946-X ● [1.Cats—Fiction. 2. Dogs—Fiction. 3. Competition (Psychology)—Fiction.] I. Title. ● PZ7.T8577Co 2005 ● [E]—dc22 ● 2003026063

I stay out late.

I'M A MEMBER OF THE KENNEL CLUB.

COOL CAT, HOT DOG

SCRAP-BOOK
a ~~condensed journal~~ based on real events
and brought to your attention by
SANDY TURNER

Atheneum Books for Young Readers

New York London Toronto Sydney

I'm Cat. I'm feline.

I'm Dog. I'm canine.

You're as ugly as a Pekingese.

You sure ain't no Siamese.

I do as I want.

I catch. I do as I'm told.

I chase leaves.

I chase thieves.

I've got fleas.

Mine are itchier.

I've got scratchy claws.

I've got padded paws.

I'm a daredevil.

I fetch.

I play the fiddle.

I howl at the moon.

I stalk mice.

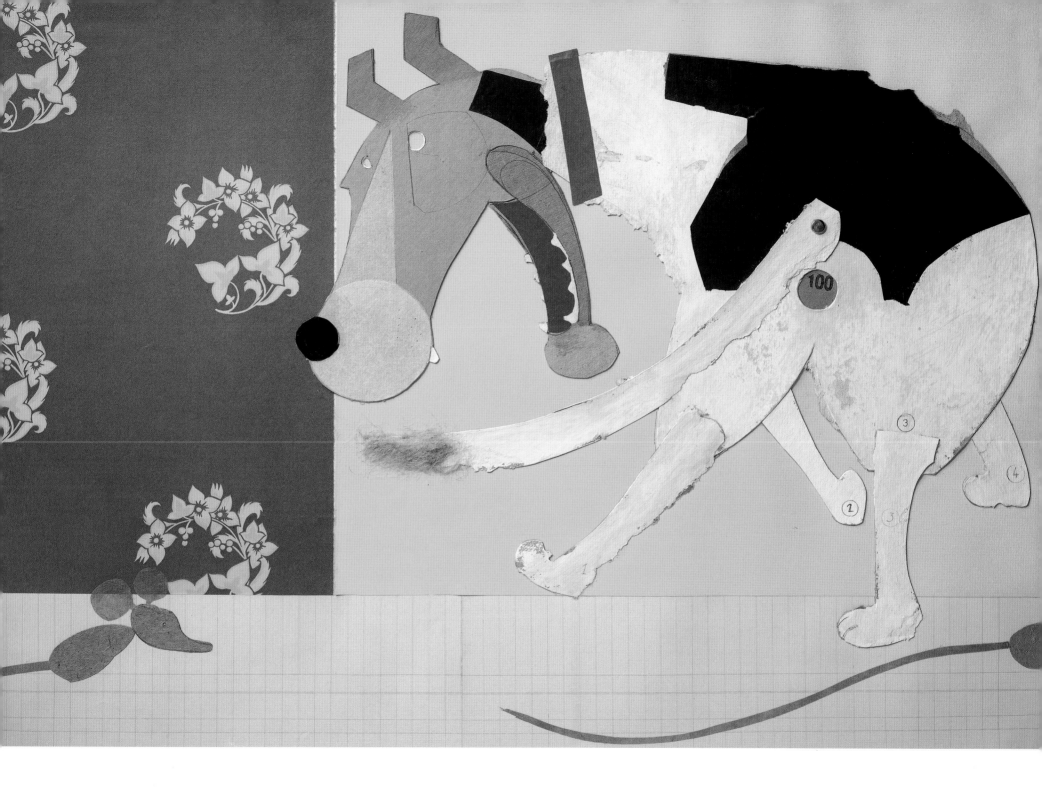

I chase my tail.

I chew grass.

I bite. (I might . . .)

I can see in the dark.

I roll around in the park.

I'm pussy—I purr.

I'm hound—I pant and drool.

I'm crafty.

I'm cunning.

My tongue is rough. My nose is pink.

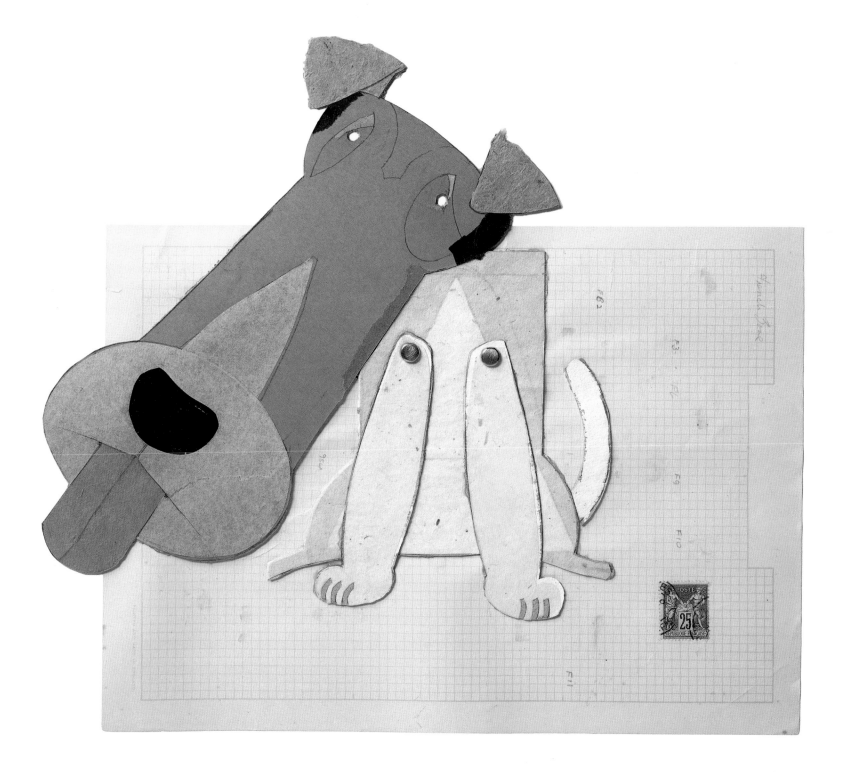

My tongue is smooth. My snout is black.

My tail is long and fluffy.

My tail is short and stumpy.

I'm mysterious. I've an independent nature.

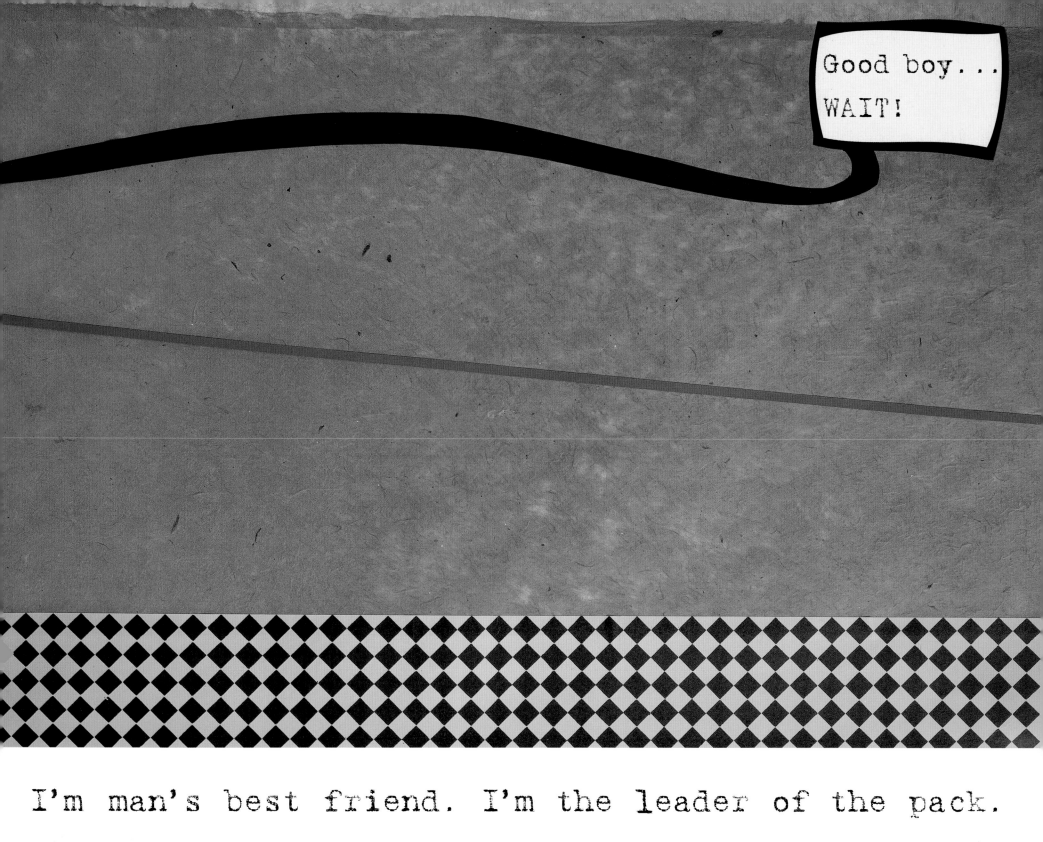

I'm man's best friend. I'm the leader of the pack.

I meow. I'm cool.

I prefer to bark. I'm hot.

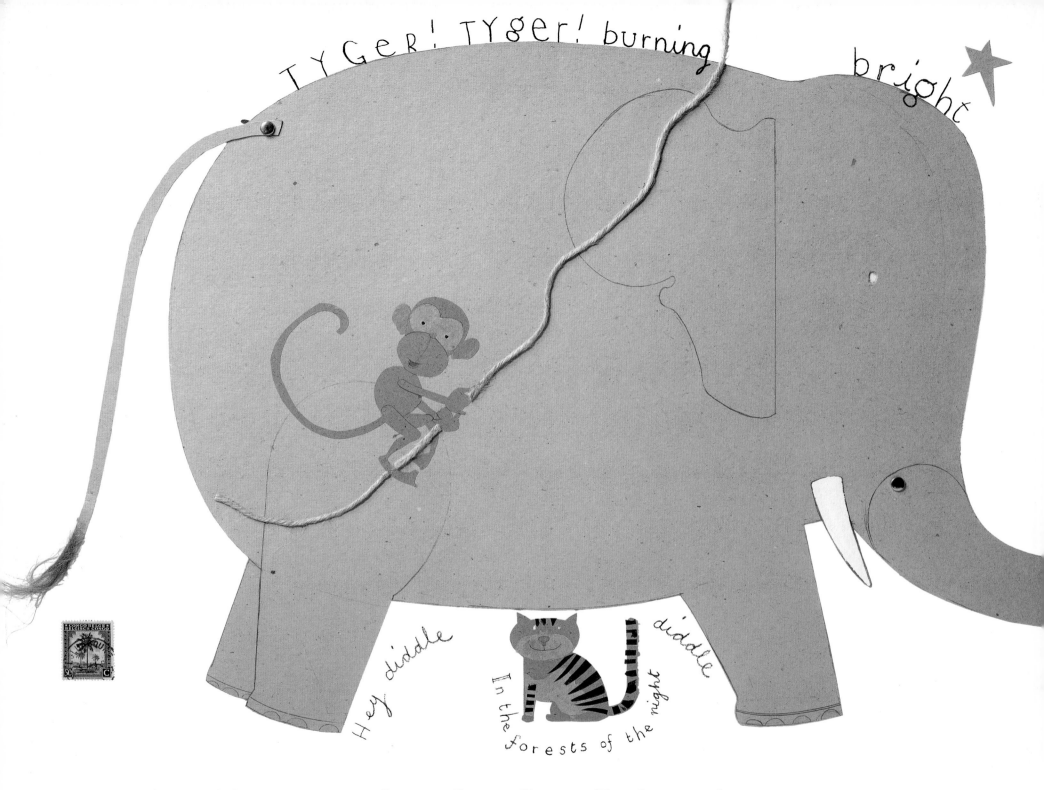

I'm King of the Jungle–I inspire poetry.

I define loyalty.

I ate a canary once.

I could eat a . . .

I'm a cool, cool cat.

I'm a hot, hot dog.